W9-BGD-976

Where Does The Sun Go At Night?

It was a splendid summer evening, and Pooh was playing tag with his friends.

"You're *it*!" shouted Roo, tagging Tigger in mid-bounce.

"Hoo-hoo-hoo!" cried Tigger. "Now I'll get Pooh!"

Tigger bounced into the darkening shadows—and straight into a bush!
"It sure complickerates this tag business when you can't see where
you're going," he said, pulling leaves from his tail.
            "What are you talking about—OOMPH!" grunted Rabbit
            as he tripped on a tree root and landed on top of Tigger.
            "Looks like you're it, Long Ears!" Tigger
            said triumphantly.

Just then, Kanga appeared in the doorway.

"It's getting dark," she called. "Time to come inside for the sleeping part of this sleep-over party."

"Awww, Mama," said Roo. "Just a few more minutes?"

Kanga shook her head and smiled.
"I've made you all a little snack. Come and get some
cookies while they're still warm."

"Why does it have to get dark?" Roo asked as he and his friends ate their way through a big plate of Kanga's delicious honey cookies.

"Mmph guf erf ucherz ur ung mmmph ewau," Pooh said.

"I beg your pardon, Pooh?" said Roo.

"Oh, bother," said Pooh. "My words got crowded out by cookies. I said that it gets dark because the sun goes away."

"But it always comes back, doesn't it, Pooh?" Piglet asked nervously.

"Yes, Piglet," answered Pooh. "Always."

"What I'd like to know is where does the sun go at night?" said Roo. "It always seems to leave just when we're having the most fun."

"We'll probably never know where it goes," Eeyore said sadly.

"We could try to find out," Piglet said. "All of us together."

"I'm with you, Buddy Boy!" Tigger said. "Then maybe we can persuaderate the sun to stay around more."

"So we wouldn't have to sleep so much," yawned Roo.

"And we could stay up playing tag all night long," said Pooh, just before he began to snore.

In the morning, the friends put their heads together to try to solve the mystery of the disappearing sun.

"First things first," Tigger said. "Where was the sun the last time we saw it?"

"I believe it was over there," Pooh said, pointing toward the field.

"No, no," Rabbit insisted. "It was over there."

"Oh, I wish I'd been watching," wailed Roo.

"I remember where it was," Piglet said quietly. "I stopped to watch it set behind the hill."

"Good work, Buddy Boy!" Tigger said. "Let's go see if it's still there!"

"It won't be," Eeyore said.

"Why not?" asked Roo.

"Because it's shining on the pond behind you," Eeyore said.

"Very mysterious," Rabbit muttered. "How do you suppose the sun got all the way over there?"

"Maybe we'd get some clues if we followed it," Piglet suggested.

"It might be kind of fun to spy on the sun," Roo said.

"Count me in," Tigger said. "Sun-spying is what tiggers do best!"

The friends spent the day following the sun all over the Hundred-Acre Wood. Rabbit saw it peeking through his garden gate in the morning. Roo and Tigger noticed it straight overhead at lunchtime. Pooh found it behind the oak tree in the made-for-napping shade late in the afternoon.

When Eeyore reported that the sun was sliding toward the hill, Piglet, Rabbit, Roo, and Tigger hurried to catch up with it.

But when they got to the top of the hill—huffing and puffing from the climb—the sun wasn't there!

Not ready to give up, the friends looked in gopher holes and inside caves. They peered under piles of leaves and underneath boulders to see if they could find the sun's nighttime hiding place. But the sun was nowhere to be found! It had simply disappeared. Again.

While his friends were searching the hillside, Pooh was watching the sunset from his Thinking Spot when Rabbit joined him.

"The sun came up near the pond," Rabbit said, making a simple drawing in the dirt. "It was straight up in the sky at noon. And then it set behind the hill—just like it did last night."

"Where do you suppose the sun will be tomorrow morning?" Pooh asked. "Think, think, think," he said, tapping his fluff-filled head.

Rabbit looked at his drawing—and suddenly he thought he might know the answer!

Rabbit got up very early to test his theory about the morning sun. Sure enough—the sun was right where he thought it would be!

He hurried to Owl's house, where all of the friends had agreed to meet that morning.

"I have very important news!" he announced.

"The sun came up near the pond again today!" Rabbit said excitedly. "I think it travels from the pond to the hill every day! That means it starts the day in the east." He squinted at a compass on Owl's table. "And it ends the day in the west."

"Super-duperous detective work, Long Ears!" Tigger said.

"But we still don't know where the sun went last night," Roo said.

"Maybe Owl can use his night vision to follow the sun tonight," Pooh suggested.

"I can do better than that," Owl said. "I believe I have the solution to your mystery right here."

"What's the big ball got to do with anything?" Tigger asked.

"This isn't a ball, Tigger," Owl explained. "It's a globe. It shows us what the planet Earth looks like."

"Does it bounce?" Tigger asked hopefully.

"No, but it does spin," Owl said.

"The fact is that the sun didn't go anywhere last night," Owl announced dramatically, giving the globe a spin. "We did!"

"Not me," Tigger said. "I was at home all night. I fell out of bed once or twice, but other than that, I stayed put."

"We may feel like we're standing still, Tigger," Owl said. "But the Earth we live on is always turning."

"Oh, my!" Piglet said nervously. "Is that a good thing, Owl?"

Owl laughed.

"It's a wonderful and amazing thing, Piglet. Let me show you."

Owl set a lantern on his table. Then he asked Tigger and Roo to close the curtains on the windows.

"Pretend that this lantern is the sun," Owl said. "Notice that it's not moving. But watch what happens when the Earth spins next to it. When the part of the Earth we live on faces the sun, it's daytime. And when it faces away from the sun, it's night," Owl explained.

"So now do you know where the sun goes at night, little Roo?" Owl asked.

"It doesn't go anywhere!" Roo exclaimed. "It just waits for us to come back around to see it."

"Oh, I think that's just splendid," said Piglet. "Don't you?"

Be a Sun Detective!

As Roo and his friends discovered, the sun doesn't move—the Earth does. Our planet is always spinning. When our part of the Earth is facing the sun, it's daytime. When our part of the Earth is turned away from the sun, it's nighttime. As the Earth turns, the sun seems to move across the sky—from east to west. One full turn of our Earth takes about 24 hours—one day and one night.

Preschoolers learn by questioning, observing and experimenting to see how things work. Just like your friends in the Hundred-Acre Wood, you can be a sun detective. Where is the sun in the morning when you wake up? Where is it at lunchtime? Where does the sun set? (Very important note for all sun detectives: To protect your eyes, never look directly at the sun.)

Like Owl, you can do an experiment that will show you how the turning of the Earth causes night and day.

Step 1:  This experiment works best in a dark room. All you need is a flashlight and a globe or a ball. If you're using a ball, put a sticker on one spot on the ball (to mark where you live). If you're using a globe, ask someone to show you where you live.

Step 2: Shine the flashlight on the ball or globe.

Step 3: Keep the flashlight still and turn the ball.

Step 4: Notice how the flashlight lights up your part of the world when it's facing the sun. Notice how your part of the world gets dark when it's facing away from the sun. Isn't science splendid?

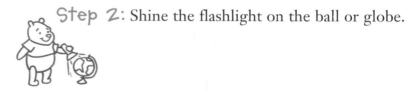